The
Perfect
Lie?

Winners of *The* **Guardian** /*Piccadilly*
teenage short story competition

The
Perfect
Lie?

Foreword by DBC PIERRE

Piccadilly Press • London

Collection copyright © Piccadilly Press, 2006
5 Castle Road, London NW1 8PR
www.piccadillypress.co.uk

Foreword © DBC Pierre
I've Never © Emma Davson, 2006
Seamlessly Fake © Kathryn Dennis-Smither, 2006
A National Hero © Rachael Flaherty, 2006
The Family Portrait © Emilie Jones, 2006
Departure © Rosie Khorshidian, 2006
Innocent Deceit © Rebecca Pedelty, 2006
Basketball ©Alison Ritchie, 2006
The Versatility of Maria © Jasmine Singh, 2006
The Life-Like-Lie © Saranja Sivachelvam, 2006
The Businessman © Conrad Steel, 2006

The right of Emma Davson, Kathryn Dennis-Smither,
Rachael Flaherty, Emilie Jones, Rosie Khorshidian,
Rebecca Pedelty, Alison Ritchie, Jasmine Singh,
Saranja Sivachelvam and Conrad Steel to be identified as
Authors of this work has been asserted by them in accordance
with the Copyright, Designs and Patents Act 1988

A catalogue record for this book is available from the British Library

ISBN: 1 85340 884 0 (trade paperback)
ISBN-13: 978 1 85340 884 7

1 3 5 7 9 10 8 6 4 2

Printed and bound in Great Britain by Bookmarque Ltd
Cover design by Simon Davis
Typeset by Textype Typesetters, Cambridge
Set in Justlefthand and Meridian

Contents

Foreword   *viii*

I've Never   *1*
EMMA DAVSON

Seamlessly Fake   *13*
KATHRYN DENNIS-SMITHER

A National Hero   *29*
RACHAEL FLAHERTY

The Family Portrait   *37*
EMILIE JONES

Departure   *47*
ROSIE KHORSHIDIAN

Innocent Deceit   *67*
REBECCA PEDELTY

Basketball   *79*
ALISON RITCHIE

The Versatility of Maria   89
JASMINE SINGH

The Lie-Like-Life   99
SARANJA SIVACHELVAM

The Businessman   107
CONRAD STEEL

Foreword

DBC Pierre

Talk about missing the boat. If only I – instead of building alternative realities to colour my school days – had written some stories. When your everyday world is half fiction, half fact, grand things can arise from knowing which half is which, and mastering each in its own habitat.

The young seem to grasp the rudiments of this.

Some of them, at least.

Apart from the admiration with which we judges read this bright assortment of works, I felt a genuine curiosity: what possessed these young minds to deploy themselves in the service of literature, when surely there was miscreance and chaos awaiting their attention on the streets?

Could it be they were *getting things together*?

These short stories answer emphatically. Perhaps teenagers are better able to map the boundaries of fiction in reality, and reality in fiction. Perhaps they can smell a fib as light as a fly's wing in an everyday transaction, and still surrender to the wildest twists of fantasy in art. Combine these traits with energy, talent and an innate sense of living through the heart of life's power-band – and we're forced to ask if any work could truly be more contemporary.

I hope you enjoy Britain's newest authors as much as we did.

I've Never

Emma Davson

I've Never

Henry settled back in his armchair and calmly surveyed the room. Pangbourne Retirement Home had done unusually well this year in its Christmas decorations, he thought. In place of the usual lurid green plastic tree stood a real fir, which emitted a rich and musty smell into the stale, over-circulated air. The off-white stucco of the ceiling was festooned with paper chains so the peeling damp patches were masked well. For the first time, Henry felt happy to be spending his Christmas there, amongst the bowls of ancient pot pourri and occasional ripples of laughter.

Usually the nurses kept the residents to a strict curfew, but tonight, Christmas Eve, they had seemingly disappeared, and their absence had caused a slightly anarchic air of abandon to spread over Henry's companions. A tape of wartime Christmas classics had been put on, and many were singing along with shaky gusto. Henry was too young to remember the songs, but he still closed his eyes and let himself be engulfed by the wave of their nostalgia.

He cast his mind back to the Christmases spent alone with Mother. Seeing as it was just the two of them, she could afford the most indulgent food and exotic toys fresh from Hamleys for Henry. Each year was a repeat of the last; he would lose himself in a game with his new train set, racing car or miniature army, while Mother would sip gin until she was out of the room in a different place, crying about her lost lover, 'Claude'. Remembering Mother like this caused Henry to feel a pang of unease, so he focused his attention on the man sitting opposite him, Jerrod, who had produced a bottle of nameless liquid and was looking mischievously about the room to see if anyone else had noticed.

Henry cleared his throat. 'What's that you've got then, Jerrod?'

Jerrod winked. The joker of the residence, he was renowned for being by far the most subversive of the group, tricking his seething nurses and refusing to take his medicine. 'The lazy girls just want me to spend the day knocked out so they don't have to bother with me,' he had said when asked why he wouldn't take his beta-blockers. He had suffered a heart attack some time before, and had hitherto been forbidden any form of intoxicants or rich foods or, as he put it, 'enjoying what's left of my life'.

More attention turned to Jerrod's bottle.

'Oooh, is that whiskey?' gasped Rita in her grating sandpaper voice.

'I've been saving it,' he said with relish, a twinkle in his eyes. 'Thought we might have a bit of *fun* for a change. It is Christmas, if any of you have forgotten!'

Henry hadn't drunk since his drinking partner had died and realised how much he could do with a tot of the stuff.

'Shall we share it out?' asked Rita, looking at the bottle with greed.

'I have a much better idea, Rita my friend, one

that you in particular will simply adore.'

The room had been rendered to silence, and all eyes were on Jerrod. His ideas, though good, were potentially hazardous. After a sufficient pause, he said, 'Does anyone remember the drinking game "I've Never"?'

There was a small ripple of recognition.

'That old game!' exclaimed Elsie. 'We played that in the WRNS!'

It wasn't something Henry was familiar with. Well, he supposed, it wasn't that surprising. He hadn't mixed with many of the rebellious types at boarding school. In fact, he hadn't mixed with many people at all, spending most of his time with his arithmetic.

Jerrod had an explanation at the ready.

'You all know the story of how I got expelled from Eton for setting fire to an unexploded bomb, I presume,' he said. This was a story that had been told countless times and it was imprinted into the minds of all the residents and even the nurses, as Jerrod was extremely fond of telling it.

Rita mock-clutched her heart in pain and exclaimed, 'No, not again!'

'Don't worry, Rita!' laughed Jerrod. 'Now, in the game, what I would do is say: "I've never been expelled from Eton for setting fire to an unexploded bomb". Now seeing as that is a dirty great lie, I and anyone else who has perpetrated that specific act have to take a penalty shot of whiskey . . .'

His eyes rolled as he took a hearty gulp and continued, '. . . for being such a sinner.' He took such delight in the word *sinner* that everybody laughed, and the game was commenced.

Rita started. 'I've never married purely for money!' she cried piercingly.

Everybody knew the history of Rita's marriages, five in all, each ending in the husband's heartbreak and Rita's swelling bank balance.

'Rita, you are terrible,' uttered Elsie as she took a swig and handed the bottle to Barnaby.

Barnaby was a civil and mild-mannered man who spoke rarely, but when he did, it was with the driest sense of humour. He passed the bottle from hand to hand and a smile played about his face as he said, 'I've never been issued with a new identity by the police.'

This caused a ripple of excitement through Henry's friends. Barnaby, however, did not further this story, much to the dismay of his curious and mildly alarmed cohorts. Knowing that Barnaby's silence was a serious one that could not be broken, as he was well-meaning but obstinate, the game was once again resumed, with a new-found inspiration. Everyone was baying for a go, but the bottle was handed around in a circle.

Henry swallowed and bit his fingernails; a habit that he could not control which had been with him since he was young and his father had left.

As cries of 'I've never ridden horseback naked!' and 'I've never climbed Mount Everest!' erupted like shining new boils on the usually placid group, Henry searched his logical accountant's mind through the years for something to say. The bottle would be with him soon, in his hands – his bitten, trembling hands.

'I've never won a fist fight!' was one which provoked several of the male members of the home (and Rita) to have to take another punishment shot.

But Henry had never fought back when he was kicked and flogged at school, and the pubs he had graced never had the sorts of people that would start a brawl.

His weak heartbeat fluttered as he saw the bottle,

now two people away. The raucous din was making him dizzy. What had he done as a young man, in his prime? Looked after Mother, before he got his first accountancy job.

'Henry!' roared Jerrod, overflowing with whiskey-induced festive exuberance. 'Pay attention, it's your turn!'

The bottle fell into his hands, like the heavy thud of a mallet marking a court sentence.

'Any skeletons in the closet?' barked Jerrod, his small eyes streaming with pleasure. 'We have so far learned that Charles escaped a POW camp, Mary was a mistress of the famed Albert Finney, and Susan published a racy novel in America under the pseudonym Sally Bridewell!'

Everyone but Henry was lost in the bizarre hilarity. As he felt the warm bottle, he had the same crashing sensation as he had had when his mother turned up at his school open day drunk and dishevelled and calling for him.

'Come on, Henry! We won't judge you!' insisted Rita.

His frail heart palpitating, he opened his mouth and said it.

'I've never come top in the chartered accountancy exam.' There. It was done. The line he had been mentally practising as rigorously as he did elaborate sums as a boy. His one jewel of pride.

He had mumbled it somewhat incoherently, but everyone had heard. Taking a wincing sip of the foul liquid, he turned away in shame. A couple of women tittered, and a song he alone didn't recognise played in the unsure silence.

'Is that the best you can do?' Jerrod laughed, his big, ruddy face curved in mockery.

Henry opened his mouth to say something better, something truly funny, an original anecdote salvaged from his past – a hastily-manufactured lie, even.

But it was too late. The game had moved on to those worthy of it. They had forgotten Henry.

Slowly and unnoticed, he eased himself out of his chair and made his way out of the room and into the endless disinfectant-smelling corridors. The garish and lurid wallpaper seemed to be jeering at him, mocking his blandness. He moved quicker than his stiffly faltering body usually allowed him so as to escape the sound of a celebration of interesting and fulfilled lives.

His room seemed emptier than before. Anger and shame rippled through his nerves as his eyes rested upon the only thing on the bare, beige walls: his accountancy certificate. How silly it looked, stark and alone, framed cheaply.

He threw it to the floor, hoping it would smash, but it merely fell the right way up and glared at him, defiant and unbroken, determined to show the world his pitiful achievement. The numbers behind it, the ones he used to love, now echoed the structure of the life he had led, never straying from his set routine.

His room was so bare it resembled a prison cell. Nothing he owned told a story or gave any insight into the person he was. *Maybe,* winced Henry, *maybe that is because there is nothing to me at all.*

He lay on his bed and remembered when James, his old drinking partner from the accountancy department, had died. James had done a number of things before he came to the business, and acquired a number of friends that regarded him with the utmost respect. His funeral was particularly well turned out, Henry being only one in a significant and varied crowd of mourners.

He imagined his own death, the one that every second of his life counted down to. Who would come to his funeral? What would they find to say? The mark he had left on the world was as faded and unremarkable as his certificate.

A plane roared overhead, and Henry imagined the people inside it, with families, or alone, anticipating adventures he was too late ever to go on himself.

Lying in bed, he wished for sleep to come and relieve him from the unbearable torment soon. As he turned to switch out the light, his eyes fell upon a picture of his great nephew, Timothy. With a lurch he remembered that Timothy would be visiting him tomorrow. If it were Jerrod he was visiting, young Timothy would be properly entertained that Christmas Day, shrieking at his playful jokes and anecdotes, hanging on to his every word.

He heard Jerrod's booming voice now, and a bubble of muted laughter beneath it. He knew that Timothy would not enjoy his visit.

Henry had no stories to tell.

seamlessly Fake

Kathryn Dennis-Smither

seamlessly Fake

The shouting goes on and on, until all I want to do is clap my hands over my ears and make it stop.

'Gay boy!'

'Faggot!'

That's me, yelling those words. I couldn't tell you why I'm shouting, except maybe because everyone else seems to be, and if I don't, they'll notice. I guess that's the same reason why, earlier, I hit this boy until he fell down, and why I kicked him once he was there. It seems like a poor excuse, even when I say it to myself.

If you asked any of the others, they would probably

give you the same reason. Why are we running after this boy? Because he's clever and works hard at school? Because he wouldn't hit back when we grabbed him? Because he didn't struggle as we broke his glasses and emptied out his bag? I guess those are the reasons. Not necessarily because he's gay, like we're yelling. I've seen him with a few girls at school, and that's pretty much all I know about him. His name is Will, and I doubt that he's gay.

My name is Zach, and I am.

Not that anyone knows, of course, least of all the boys around me. We've stopped running now, because Will seems to have disappeared, which I'm glad of. There are five of us, and we did him a lot of damage just now, so I don't know what would have happened if we'd caught him. I guess the same that would happen to me if I turned around right now and went, 'Hey, I'm gay, did you know?' They'd fit what was left of me into a matchbox.

We've been tormenting this boy for weeks. I can't remember what started it; maybe he spoke back to one of us, or maybe he just looked at us in the wrong way. All I know is that we've been following him home every day for the past few weeks, and he's done nothing about it. I don't know why; it's like he doesn't care, or he can't be bothered to stop us. I know that if I was him, I would be shit-scared of what we would do tomorrow, knowing that every day it can only get worse.

The others are squashed on a bench, having a smoke, but there's no room for me, so I make some excuse and start walking home. I seem to spend my life making excuses: why I'm late to school; why I haven't done my work; why I join in when they beat up that boy; why I won't tell anyone my ever-growing secret.

I want to tell someone, I do. But who would I tell? I'd get crucified if I told anyone at school, I know that much. My family would never understand. My brother's the ultimate heterosexual male: weight-lifter, chain-smoker, serial womaniser. I've never told him anything personal in my life – not since I was ten, and then he informed all my friends that I couldn't sleep without the light on. My dad thinks he's the perfect son, and I'm just the disappointing younger child. There's nothing that I can do that Brian hasn't done before me. Dad would probably try to 'straighten me out', and I'd end up eating boiled cabbage and having cold showers until I'm thirty, when he'd finally give up and disown me. And Mum . . . well, she left a note and walked out three years ago, and none of us have heard from her since. I don't think about her much.

I hate living this lie. All the time, I have to act, in case I forget who I'm supposed to be and let something slip. I'm good at it though; pretending to be someone that I'm not. Who would ever suspect that I'm gay? I'm Zach Solomon, football captain, sports fanatic, three girlfriends in the last six months. That's me, but it's as if there's a whole other me just under the surface, that keeps trying to claw its way out. I just have to keep suppressing it. Hell, maybe I should just give up football and go into acting. I seem to be better at pretending to be someone I'm not than anything else.

I know that eventually I'll have to come out to the world, but I don't know if I can face it. You saw what the boys back there were like; if they found out, they'd turn on me. I'm terrified of what people would think, or say, or do.

Every morning I get up and tell myself that, today, I will come clean to everyone: my father, my brother and my friends. But then I look at myself in the mirror, and think: *I'm gay. I'm what millions of people hate. I'm what they protest about. Everywhere I go, there will be someone who hates me for being me.* So I tell no one, and I spend the day hanging around with my 'friends' back there, chasing people like Will and being someone that I can't stand.

I don't know any other gay people, or anyone that I could turn to for help. I'm on my own. I don't think that I could handle coming out, and being even more scared than I am now. After all, there's nothing worse than being afraid and alone.

I don't know when it started. I didn't wake up one morning, and think: *Blimey! I like boys!* I've always been like this. I never really noticed it. I can remember the moment that I realised; I was on the train, on my way to a football trial, watching a couple that were sitting across from me, kissing. I was looking at the girl, and thinking about what it would be like to be the bloke, kissing her, and then moved on to thinking about what it would be like to be her, kissing him. From then on it's all a kind of blur, like I was caught in a rush of feeling, because that's when I finally realised that I was gay. It was as if all the signs had been pointing in that direction, and I'd only just figured out where they were leading me.

I botched the football trial because I was so messed up, and my dad yelled at me when I got home. When he bellowed at me, 'What the hell was going on in your head?' I told my first lie about myself, and it's carried on from there.

I just wish it would stop. Or that I was someone else. My dream is that one day, I'll just leave the house, get on the train, and go anywhere that isn't here. I'll start a whole new life for myself, and just be me.

I'm not looking where I'm going, because I'm lost in my thoughts, so I walk into someone coming the other way. He drops the pile of books that he's carrying and, without looking at him, I pick them up. As I straighten up to hand them to him, I realise who he is: Will – the boy who, half an hour ago, I hit in the face. I don't know what to do, so I silently pass him his books.

'Thanks,' he says, smiling at me. He has a nice smile, I realise; he's looking at me as if he's forgotten that I was the one who made that cut on his cheek.

Then he recognises me, and the smile fades.

I can't think of anything to say, so I mutter, 'S'all right,' and walk on. I go perhaps ten paces and then abruptly turn around.

'Don't you care?' I call to his retreating back.

He stops walking and slowly spins around to face me. 'Care about what?' he asks calmly. He has a hostile look in his eyes, but he doesn't seem afraid.

'What we do to you! What I do! Don't you hate me?' I can't understand why it doesn't seem to bother him like it would bother me.

He's smiling again as he walks back towards me; that smile, disarming and open, as if I'd never done anything to hurt him. 'No,' he says as he stops, facing me. 'I would do, only I don't think that you were really enjoying it either.'

I have no idea what to say, so I just gape at him.

'Why do you do it?' he asks, still looking me straight in the eyes.

I come dangerously close to blurting it all out, so I break eye contact and stare instead at the books in his arms; they are dirty and ripped, and one of them is missing a cover. I remember how, earlier, we pulled the pages out of a couple of them. I scuff the ground with my foot and shrug, like I do when my dad shouts at me about my botched football trials, or when I mention Mum.

'I mean, you're not like the rest of them. You don't seem to want to hurt me, like they do.' He shrugs too, the smile gone. 'When they lay into me, you always seem to hold back. Why do you hang around with them?'

I shrug again. I barely know how to explain my actions to myself, let alone someone else.

'You follow me home with them, and you yell insults, and you call me gay and poofter and faggot, but you don't mean it. What are you, in denial?' The smile is back, like it's a joke and it's a ridiculous idea.

I want to yell an answer at him, because I can't let him find out but my throat seems to have seized up, and all I can manage is a hoarse, 'No!'

I realise immediately what I've done, and slowly look back up from the books and straight into his eyes. He stops smiling and his eyes widen, and I know that he's realised.

I wait for disgust, or outrage, or maybe even anger. But none of that happens. 'Oh, Christ,' he says softly. 'You're gay, aren't you?'

Without waiting for an answer, he just bursts out laughing, like I've made some amazing joke. 'Unbelievable!' he laughs. 'You complete fool! You're such an idiot!'

He's laughing so hard that he drops his books again, and then sits down hard on the pavement, cackling like a lunatic.

I stare down at him in disbelief. How can he think that this is funny? This is my life that he's laughing about! This is me that he finds so hilarious! Yet his laughter is infectious, and I can't help but smile at him rolling on the ground. He grabs my arm and pulls me down with him, as he stops laughing and catches his breath.

'So this whole masquerade that you've been putting on has just been a way to avoid coming out?' he asks, his eyes not mocking, but still full of laughter. 'I've had to put up with you punching me in the face just because you've got this denial thing?'

I avoid his eyes again. The way that he says it makes it all sound so stupid.

'Oh come on, Zach.' I glance up, not realising that he knew my name, to see him looking at me, sombre once more. 'It's not like people care.'

'People care,' I say shortly. I should have known that he wouldn't understand.

'OK, some people care,' he concedes. 'But does it really matter what they think?'

'That lot back there,' I say, knowing that he'll understand who I mean. 'They'll hate me.'

'So what?' he asks. 'Do you want people like that to like you? Do you really want to spend the rest of your life trying to be someone that you're not, just to please a load of bigots?'

I look at him, trying to figure out if he means what he's saying. Ever since I realised that I was gay, I'd always assumed that the majority of people would hate me for it. I know that my dad would kick me out, and where would I go then? Ever since Mum left, the thing that I've been most afraid of in the world is being alone. If I came out, I'd be outcast by the people that I know now. My dad and my brother would have nothing to do with me, and it's not like I have any friends who would understand. I'd be a complete outsider, just for being me, and I would be even more alone than I am now.

But would I? I'm not alone now, am I? I'm sitting here, collapsed on the pavement with Will, who most certainly doesn't seem to hate me for being me. The smile that I'm wearing now is the first genuine one that I've worn for months.

He's watching me like I'm having an epiphany. Which, I suppose, is one way of describing it. I grin at him, and he smiles back and pokes me on the arm.

'See?' he says, smiling that disarming smile, his eyes full of a brilliant 'I'm right and you're wrong' quality. 'The whole world isn't against you.'

Then his eyes slide past me and his face changes. Before I can turn to see what it is that he's looking at, he grabs my arm and pulls me to my feet.

The boys, who half an hour ago I'd left sitting on a bench, smoking, are walking along the road towards us. The boys, who, if they knew the content of the conversation I'd just had with Will, would quite possibly kill me. The boys who will probably attack me for having any kind of conversation with him.

I look at Will. I don't know what to do. If I turn against him now, I could lose the only real friend I've got. But if I stand up for myself against the approaching boys, anything might happen to us. I wouldn't blame Will if he turned and ran, leaving me to deal with this on my own. But he's watching the boys with a resolute, almost calm, look, even though he's gripped my arm like a vice. 'I think it's time for some truth-telling, don't you?' he says quietly.

The boys reach us, and one of them kicks Will's books out of the way. 'Enjoying spending time with the faggot?' he asks me, staring threateningly at Will.

I open my mouth to reply, and realise that I don't know what to say. What *can* I say?

Will has seen me freeze, because he takes control. 'Yes,' he says coolly. 'I am.'

They don't understand. You can see their faces, trying to work out what he means. I must have put on a pretty convincing act during the time that I spent with them. Looking back on it, I can't remember what reason I gave myself to justify spending any time with them.

Finally, it filters through. 'Oi, Zach!' one of them grunts. 'He just called you gay!'

Out of the corner of my eye, I see Will open his mouth to reply, but I decide that this is something that I need to do. 'Well, that's interesting, isn't it?' I say, hardly believing that this is the moment that I've been dreading for so long. 'Because he's right.'

seamlessly Fake

In that moment, I see their expressions change from threatening to plain angry, and as one of them starts towards us, I grab Will, spin him around, and pull him into a run.

I can hear their footsteps pounding behind us, and I know that they're catching up. Part of me is terrified, but the rest of me doesn't care; I can't help but give in to the elated feeling that's rushing up inside of me. *I've done it. I'm out, and there's nothing that anyone can throw at me that I can't stand.*

Except then I hear the click of a flick-knife in the hand of one of the boys following us. I know that Will has heard it too; we both automatically run faster – but where we're going, I don't know.

I'm afraid, so I keep running. I glance at Will; he's staring straight ahead, concentrating on where he's going, his cheeks red, breathing hard. Somehow, knowing that he is beside me makes me less scared. If I have to run, at least I have someone to run with. After all, there's nothing worse than being afraid and alone.

A National Hero

Rachael Flaherty

A National Hero

Come on, join up today *and you will be a hero. You will be covered in glory. For king and country! For freedom! Sign up today and you could make the difference. We need YOU!* That's what the posters said. That's what the government said. And that's what I believed!

When I signed up I knew it was my duty to fight for king and country; to show how patriotic I was. That I would do anything – and I mean anything – even sacrifice my life. I *knew* I was doing the right thing.

We read those posters. We heard the talk. We asked no questions. Why should we?

How well it all began. Billy, Freddy and me,

tramping out of the factory after another boring, backbreaking shift. I had worked there five years, but never got used to it. It really was like hell. Why should I have to work so hard with only a couple of shillings to show for it in my torn back pocket, when those posh blokes just sat behind a desk all day drinking tea and getting hundreds. Anyway, we were on our way to the football pitch for a quick kick-about before tea, when we came across this fella, out recruiting for the army.

We all looked at each other and I knew we were thinking the same thing. This would be different. This would be exciting. Something worth living for. We'd make our folks proud. And when we came back we'd be men, and the birds would fall at our feet. But at least if we didn't come back, we'd be heroes! And let's not forget – those Germans needed to be taught a good lesson, threatening our peace and our freedom.

So Billy, Freddy and me took the king's shilling and we were happy to do so.

At the time I thought it was the best day of my life. Now I wish that day had never happened. What a mistake it was.

The letter came through soon enough, telling us

when we were leaving. Mum went round telling everyone on the street about it. Time flew by after that. It was all we ever talked about, and poor Mum was so proud. Before we knew it there we were, kitted out in our uniforms and ready to go.

Then came the day when we had to say our goodbyes. We felt so marvellous, marching off. Folks lined the street, three deep in some places, waving flags and banners and cheering for all they were worth. They were all dressed in their best clothes and all the gals were chucking flowers at us. It was great! I could hear the band playing songs: stirring songs, patriotic songs, songs we sang down the pub on a Saturday night. I particularly remember 'It's a Long Way to Tipperary', it was one of my favourites.

The journey over the Channel was horrible. The fact we'd all had too many beers the night before didn't help. Freddy was sick overboard at least five times. I'd never been on a boat before, never been abroad. I think we all had got a bit over-excited and caught up in the moment. But our hopes were set a bit too high, like the Union Jack, fluttering overhead.

It all got serious pretty damn quick after that.

Tough talks, whipping us into shape. We had to do what the officers told us to do or we'd be punished. No more games of football for us. But still we didn't question them or mind. They were educated chaps and we put our faith in them to do their best.

Then we got to the trenches and there we'd stay until the Germans surrendered. It was horrendous. I soon realised it wasn't all it was cracked up to be and that I was on the long road to doom, not glory. Some of the boys couldn't take it and tried to walk away. The firing squad was all they got by way of a thank you.

The deafening crash of mortar bombs was neverending, and the constant screaming of men as they fell for their country was horrific. Smoke filled the air, filling our lungs and burning our eyes. The smell and sight of blood was sickening – and everywhere you turned. The constant sight of my mates on the ground, dead, was gut-wrenching. Some of them shot themselves – they couldn't bear it any longer. They knew just as well as the people in charge back home that they alone couldn't make a difference, and that they wouldn't return home a hero even if they did hang on a bit longer. Cannon-fodder is all we were.

It was so damp and cold, like a dank cellar. It was the type of cold that crept into your bones. The type of cold you could never rid yourself of; it ate into you. I don't know what was worse, that damn cold or the fear – either way you just shivered the whole time. Not surprisingly, lots of us got pneumonia. What a tough bunch of boys we were now!

All the men were long past depression. No matter what songs we sung or stories we told, nothing could lighten the mood. We knew what was waiting for us. Night after night, day after day, there was never any peace, and there was definitely no saying what you thought, what you dreamed.

If you thought it couldn't get any worse, it could. We had to go over the top. We were ordered to do it, like cattle. We had no choice and, once you were over, you just had to hope for the best. We weren't heroes, we were sacrificed like lambs. Did our country care? It didn't feel like it.

Think of something bad, then think it one hundred times worse. The factory now seemed like heaven. We were in hell.

Now I'm here, stuck in this hospital, lying on a lousy mattress with poor fellows gasping their last breaths for company. The nurses do their best, but there's just not enough of them and there isn't enough medicine to go round. I don't see any reason why someone would come here in their right mind – although on second thoughts, I did exactly the same as them, wanting to be a national hero, and becoming a national embarrassment. My legs blown away, disfigured. I don't want to think about what's happened to Billy and Freddy. All I can tell is I miss them. What am I going to tell their folks when I get back – even in this sorry state – and they don't? We were friends, meant to stick together.

I dunno how long I'm going to be here, but I don't want to go home either. I'll just be a burden. I'm good for nothing. I can't even work in the factory, and no girl's going to want to know me. I'm not going to have a hero's welcome when I get back. I'll be a laughing stock, more like.

How did I let myself believe the lie? Was I lying to myself, or was it the government's lie? A perfect lie!

The Family Portrait

Emilie Jones

The Family Portrait

What is the perfect family? A mum, young, but not too young, in a flowery dress with delicate make-up and not a hair out of place. Around her waist is her husband's arm. Dad is smiling, his white teeth on show; he wears expensive jewellery and gel in his hair, his face filled with love. His other hand rests on the shoulder of a beautiful girl with long shiny hair, olive skin, just like her sister who sits next to her – they have the same smile, the same dark, mysterious eyes.

Look harder at the picture. Look deeper into those

eyes. Now does everything look so perfect? What a good job the mother makes of bringing up her children, keeping the house immaculate. Look at her now. His teeth pierce her skin, red blood smothering the white skin. He pushes her against the wall, face filled with anger. With one hand he grabs her waist, with the other he snatches the shoulder strap of her dress; he rips it and the flowers fall to the ground as the summer sun turns to a bleak winter. Tears drag her make-up down her face; her hair is ruffled, but she doesn't care. All she wants is to escape his grasp, to escape, to be free. Free from him.

Finally, his grasp loosens. She begins to relax, until – SMACK! The blow hits her like a thousand daggers; an icy chill runs down her spine. She tries to push him away, but he won't move.

Upstairs, their eldest daughter leans out of her window; the smoke from her cigarette swirls like a tornado in the peaceful breeze. A thudding bassline hammers hard in her ears, so hard she can't think. She doesn't want to think, she's seen this too many times before.

Their youngest daughter scrambles under her bed, searching frantically for a bottle. Tears drip silently down her face. Rock music plays in the background, telling stories of confusion, of people who have lost their way, of desperation. She leans back on the cupboard and relates to every word. She takes a gulp from the bottle and grimaces. It burns the back of her throat – her attempt to cover up the pain in her heart. With every drop she feels more her. Blurred voices swirl in her head, the room spins slightly, she grasps the cupboard to keep her balance. At least now she doesn't feel hurt, just a dark cloud at the back of her mind.

In the kitchen, the woman sweeps up broken glass. She crawls round the hard floor, making sure not to miss any. She carries it to the bin. But her hands are shaky, she drops a large shard; she spots it glistening, it looks so beautiful – but as she picks it up it pricks her finger; drops of blood fall from her hand and stain the floor. She puts the glass in the bin. She picks her crumpled dress up off the floor and smoothes it out, sure she can fix it. She rubs some salt water on to the bloodstains. She scrubs and scrubs, harder and harder, willing them to fade. Eventually they do, but how long will it be before more blood is spilled? She walks quietly upstairs, thoughts whizzing through her mind, each one like a bomb being dropped. When will he be back? BANG. How are the girls coping? BANG. What's going to happen? BANG.

As she gets to the landing, she slowly pushes open the door to her youngest daughter's bedroom. The girl sleeps on top of her covers, her head resting between the wall and the bedpost, still clutching the almost-empty bottle. Her mother stares at her sadly, as she fetches a blanket and covers her child with it. The mother does not shout or even feel angry. She blames herself. She will have to be there for 'her baby'. She slips into her eldest girl's room. She too is asleep, cuddling her teddy bear so tightly, like she will never let go, tears trapped in the corners of her eyes. The window is still open and a cool breeze wafts around the room, the woman goes to shut it. She feels more pangs of guilt as she spots the ashtray hidden behind the curtains. She will say nothing. Making sure that the ashes are dead, she tips them into the bin in the corner of the room, and puts the ashtray back where she found it. She will have to be there for *both* of her children. They both need her – more than either of them realise.

Finally she steps into the shower; the water cooled her bruised body down instantly. She has two wonderful daughters who need her help so much; two beautiful, talented individuals, being damaged. She has to do something, but what? Suddenly she panics, what if he comes back now? She checks the lock on the door. It is closed. Good. She has visions of him coming back with a knife and stabbing her through the shower curtain, like in that movie. She tells herself she is being stupid, that her imagination is getting carried away. But is it? She doesn't know. She is scared, really scared; scared of not knowing what he might do next.

She gets out of the shower and scrubs herself down with the towel, being sure every last trace of blood is removed. All that remains are the bruises and scratches. She knows sleep will be elusive; she will lie there with the usual lump in her stomach, tossing and turning.

She wakes in the morning to an empty bed; he obviously has not come home. She gets up; she doesn't want breakfast, she feels too sick, but she has lots to do and cannot afford to lie in – not that she wants to anyway, as she would have only her thoughts to comfort her, and right now they are not comforting.

She heads for the bathroom, on auto-pilot, and does her daily beauty regime without really focusing on anything.

She goes downstairs and makes a cup of coffee. She sips it slowly as she walks over to the mirror. She peers at it and wonders who it is staring back. It isn't her. She reaches for her make-up bag to work on her face. First, the black eye has to go.

The youngest daughter wakes with a start; she takes quick, short breaths and is hot and sweating. She has been dreaming. She used to have great dreams of her and her family going on holiday to the seaside, or of her and her friends having a party, but these dreams are long gone. Last night she dreamed she was running and running, and not getting anywhere. Memories of the night before flood her head and she closes her eyes. She aches everywhere and has no energy, even though she has just woken up. She opens a few drawers and finally locates some paracetamol to calm her head. She swigs from the nearly-empty bottle from the bedside table to wash the tablets down. Hopefully they will start to kick in soon. She stumbles across the landing and carefully opens her sister's door. Her sister is sitting on the edge of her bed, staring out of the window. She turns around when she realises her younger sibling is standing in the doorway. Neither of them speak, they just look at each other. Finally, one smiles weakly, and the other smiles back, and they hug.

They go downstairs together to their mum. As they open the living room door they see her reflection in the mirror; she looks stunning. She's just finishing straightening her amazing locks. She smiles at them as they stand in the doorway. They have seen her transformed so many times before, but this time is especially good – not a scratch or bruise in sight.

Soon the daughters have also managed to transform themselves; not a whiff of cigarette smoke or alcohol, light make-up around their eyes to cover up any dark shadows, and false smiles plastered on their faces. The perfect lie.

They leave that morning for the shops: the perfect housewife and her perfect daughters; her perfect husband out at work, supporting his family, smiling, showing his white teeth, wearing his expensive jewellery with perfectly-gelled hair. His face filled with love as he boasts about his young wife – not too young, though! He shows people a photograph of them, his beautiful wife with delicate make-up and not a hair out of place, wearing her flowery dress. In front, his two beautiful girls with long hair and shiny olive skin, both have the same smile and the same dark, mysterious eyes.

People look at that photo every day, but they don't look hard enough, they don't look deep into those eyes.

Everything seems perfect.

Departure

Rosie Khorshidian

Departure

Adam stood on the cold platform and stared along the track. It was a cold November day and his long black hair blew around his face, so that he had to keep brushing it out of his eyes. The tracks were lightly frosted, and the sky an oppressive blue-tinged grey. The place was virtually deserted; there was only a round-bellied man with a huge scarf wrapped around his neck, and an old woman with a suitcase. Apart from them, Adam was completely alone. He stared down at his feet, feeling his heart pumping. One person kept invading his mind, insistently, whispering to him across the tracks as the leaves were blown up in the air. Sending me a kiss, Adam thought and smiled.

Less than five miles away, his friend stood on another train platform. Miles was squinting up at the electronic timetable screen; he was hopeless at understanding them. He eventually managed to work out that his train should be arriving in five minutes. He'd gone to the station outside town for specific reasons. For a while, Miles waited there patiently at the empty station, in a pair of old jeans and a faded T-shirt.

Adam

I had to jump over a puddle of yellow sick to reach the sofa where Miles and Jason were lying crashed out, dying joints still clutched in their fingers.

'Miles, wake up,' I said, shaking his shoulder gently.

'Wuuu?' He sat up groggily, rubbing his eyes. His hair stood on end and a bit of dribble ran down his chin.

'We've got to tidy up now – my parents are coming back first thing.'

He groaned, smirking slightly, stretching his arms behind him and holding the back of the sofa. 'Now?'

'Yeah – now,' I said, kicking a beer can. 'Or I am in some serious trouble.'

He giggled, curling up. 'Dude, I am so smashed.'

'I don't care, you're helping me clean this up – now.'

Grinning serenely, he wobbled to his feet, swaying slightly. Jason woke up and looked up at us blearily.

'Jason, you'd better get home, we've gotta tidy this mess up.'

'I would stay . . .' Jason began.

'Don't worry about it.'

He stumbled out, leaving Miles and me alone in the living room.

'This is going to take a while.'

The room was absolutely trashed. I'd thrown a party for my seventeenth and the whole school had turned up. An armchair was overturned, now with a hole in it, and something disgusting was dripping down the window. Cans of beer and vodka bottles were littered around the place.

Miles tottered over to me and then lurched forwards.

'Whoa,' I said, catching him under the armpits

before he fell into me. I held on to his shoulders just in case he went dizzy again. 'Right – OK. Are you OK now?'

He grinned at me, and then reached up and stroked my hair. The sudden touch sent tingles all through my body.

'Miles . . .' I began, without a clue of what I was actually going to say. I didn't know what was happening.

And then he kissed me. He brought his face down to mine and touched his lips on my lips. A split second. When he drew away he whispered, 'I love you, Adam.' Before I could speak, he had collapsed.

That was the party Miles threw for me after he'd ignored me for two years. It was also after that party that we stopped speaking for ever.

Miles

Until a month before Adam's seventeenth, I'd completely ignored him. Don't get me wrong. Adam had always meant the world to me. I wanted to speak to him, but I couldn't. I was enjoying myself. I had grown up. As time went on, it got easier to pretend he didn't matter to me.

Then one day Adam came to school and he was . . . changed. I barely recognised him. He used to have this mousy-brown mop of hair, but now he'd dyed it jet black – like mine – and styled it into this amazing spiky hairdo. He'd changed his clothes too. Instead of his usual baggy T-shirt and cords, he was wearing a band T-shirt and tight jeans. He looked the business. Everyone seemed to notice. People were saying things like 'Wow, nice hair, dude,' and girls noticed, of course. I didn't know what the hell to do. Finally, I decided to go and speak to him, and we sat together for the first time in two years.

'You know, man, you should get your lip pierced too,' I told him.

Adam

'Do you really mean that – about the lip piercing?'

We were walking home, Miles and me, just as we always used to do.

'What?'

'You said I should get my lip pierced.'

Miles shrugged. 'Yeah, well, it'd look cool. But you're scared of needles, aren't you?'

I'd certainly been scared of needles when I was

younger. I remember once Miles had to sit with me while I cried my eyes out after the TB jab in the school medical room. I still was scared of needles.

'Not any more,' I lied. 'I wanna get it done.'

'Sure, OK,' Miles said. 'We'll go on the weekend or something'.

It was Monday.

'No – I want it done today. Now,' I said. I felt breathless with excitement.

'Uh, OK then . . .' he said, sounding surprised. 'There's a place we can go in the market.'

'Let's go then.'

I'd never been in the market before. It was the indoor kind that sold fake designer watches and tacky goth clothes. Even in my new attire, I felt distinctly out of place. Loud heavy metal was blaring out of the speakers, practically shaking the rusty clothes rails. Guys were walking around in tight black trousers and eyeliner, and girls in leather skirts that just covered their pants. Miles was shouting something that I couldn't make out over the noise.

'I said OVER THERE!' he yelled, pointing.

It was this shabby-looking counter with a

luminous sign hanging overhead that read *Body Piercing*. A dirty-looking guy of about sixty was behind the counter. I began to have serious second thoughts.

'C'mon.' Miles grabbed my arm and dragged me up to the counter. 'One lip piercing please!' Miles told the dirty guy, slamming some notes on the greasy surface.

'Wait —' I began.

'Shut it, I want to pay.'

'No, I mean wait, I —'

'How old is 'ee?' the dirty guy asked Miles.

'He's eighteen.'

I was then only sixteen.

'Right, come in the back.' The guy beckoned me to come round the counter.

'Is this going to hurt?' I squeaked at Miles, who was pushing me forcibly behind the counter and through a set of ripped blood-red curtains.

'A bit,' he said and grinned as I sat on the chair.

Turned out it hurt quite a lot more than a bit, but I didn't care. I kept checking it out in shop windows as we walked back to my house.

Miles

I hadn't been back to Adam's place in two years. I can't tell you how strange that was. It was like going back in time or something. It hadn't changed much. I remembered the photos on the walls; there was this one of Adam on a rollercoaster I'd always made fun of. He didn't seem to fit in there any more, with his tight clothes and his lip piercing. Last time I'd been in there with him he'd been wearing something like a woolly jumper, for God's sake.

His room was pretty much how I remembered it as well: same boring blue walls, same quilt covers, same CD player. I remembered the countless times we'd been in there before, doing our maths homework and listening to atrocious music and talking about the sexiest girls in school. I felt strangely at home.

We sat on his bed and looked through some old school photos. There were loads of us together, and one particularly amusing one of me in a school play, which Adam cracked up over.

'Nearly your birthday, isn't it? You should have a party,' I said, checking his calendar.

'Maybe.'

Departure

Adam

Sitting alone in my room after Miles left, I couldn't
stop thinking about him. Lying on my bed, I touched
the place Miles had sat.

You can't say anything.

I felt like crying. I felt deflated, worn out,
hopeless. There is no way you can tell people some
things. But you go crazy not saying anything.

I bit my pillow, thinking about Miles's smile.

Does he know?

I couldn't believe that he could. He would have
said something, surely. Miles always said what he
felt.

Miles

Adam started acting really strange after a while.
Well, he stopped going out with us and didn't act as
friendly towards me. He always said his mum kept
him in, which I know for a fact was a lie. When I
tried to talk to him about it, he changed the subject
and pretended he didn't know what I was on about.
I didn't know what to do, so I just left him to it for a
couple of weeks. Then, watching TV one night, I
decided to call around. It was the weekend before his

seventeenth birthday, and I realised that I had promised him a party.

I thought he wasn't going to answer the door at first. I rang the doorbell a couple of times with no answer. I stood on the porch, shivering and wondering if it was a bad idea, whether to just go on home. Then he answered it.

He came to the door wearing this old baggy T-shirt and slippers.

'Oh . . .' he said.

'Hey, Adam,' I said quickly. 'I was just passing and I thought we could talk about your birthday party.'

'My what?'

'Uh, well, it's your birthday next week, isn't it? And I said you should throw a party.'

'I don't know. I don't know if I'll be allowed.'

'Come on, Adam – you said your parents were going away or something?'

'Yeah, but not on my birthday.'

'So we can have it when they *do* go away, right?'

'Uh . . .'

Adam stood in the doorway the whole time. He never asked me in.

'OK, I'll think about it,' he said at last, but he didn't look exactly enthusiastic.

'We'll talk about it at school. It'll be great,' I said. And he closed the door.

The party went ahead. It started at seven o'clock and Adam, in his new birthday clothes, was thoroughly enjoying the role of host.

'C'mon, Adam, let's grab a drink,' I said, as people carried on arriving.

'But I'm the host,' he said, smirking at a group of ogling girls.

'Sod that, come on.'

He came in the end, but after much wheedling on my part. *The little prat*, I thought. *He loves being more popular than I am for once.*

When we arrived in the kitchen, I was still in a bit of a huff.

'Cheer up, grumpy guts,' Adam said. He tossed me a beer, which I downed quickly. Moving furniture is thirsty work. He had one, and then he asked me to dance with him.

'What!' I said.

'Come on, Miles.' He grabbed me and began

twirling me about madly to this heavy metal music.

'Adam . . .' I began, but stopped complaining after a while. It was quite fun, and the beer was going to my head. He was quite a good dancer, really. He pulled me up on to the kitchen counter and we danced on that for a while, to excited hoots from people milling about below us. I was waving my arms about wildly, when I caught the light above us and it broke.

'Oh God!' A few shards of glass fell on the counter, at our feet.

'Don't worry about it,' Adam said, laughing. He grabbed my arms and pulled me close to him and we carried on jumping up and down, screaming.

I began to notice how pretty he looked with his hair flopping about and his teeth gleaming. We slurped another couple of cans as we danced up there. I started to feel a bit sick.

'Hey man, I think I better get down . . .' I toppled off the counter before I could say much else, in a giggling mess on the kitchen floor. Adam hopped off, laughing, to see if I was all right.

'Faggot,' he said, handing me some kitchen roll to clear up my dribble.

The night went on and I left Adam for a bit to talk

to some people. It wasn't like he was on his own; in fact he was virtually surrounded by adoring girls on the sofa. I started to get a bit annoyed, so I just carried on drinking. My mate, Jason, rolled a few joints and I smoked a few, my stomach feeling worse and worse every minute.

Soon I felt really sick and groped my way over the writhing bodies on the floor to get to the bathroom. Someone was already in there, so I had to sit outside with my head in my hands until they came out. I was sick the minute I got in there; most of it went in the toilet but a few splashes caught the bathroom tiles.

I didn't feel much better afterwards. I crawled out and flopped on the sofa. Jason offered me another joint. I firmly refused it at first, but then I looked around and saw Adam going upstairs with this girl wound around him, and I took it.

Soon after, I fell asleep.

I was woken up by Adam, shaking my shoulder. I opened my eyes to see his face swimming above me. He said something like, 'Miles, we have to tidy this mess up.' I felt really stupid and giggly, and just laughed. Jason, who'd been on the sofa with me, woke up and left. The living room was empty. So it was just Adam and me.

He went into the kitchen to get cleaning stuff or something. I followed him, tripping over my feet and staggering. I rested up against the counter we'd been dancing on, feeling ridiculously cheerful. I watched him getting together the bin bags and disinfectant, admiring him. I kept thinking that he just looked so cute.

He started to get a bit annoyed that I wasn't doing anything, so I thought I'd walk over. I ended up stumbling and nearly falling, but he caught me under the armpits and propped me up on my feet.

On impulse, I reached up and stroked his hair. He half closed his eyes and mumbled my name.

Then I did something stupid and kissed Adam right on his lips. I don't remember anything after that, so I must have passed out.

After the party, I went back to completely ignoring him at school. Whenever he tried to approach me, I covered my ears with my hands like a little kid and ran off. Then one day I was eating lunch with my friends in the cafeteria and he walked past, carrying his burger and chips. I couldn't help it, I stared after him. Jason, seeing me looking, said, 'Oh yeah, I was meaning to ask you – do you fancy Adam or something?'

Everyone around the table was silent. I blinked for a moment, and Adam heard, of course, and looked at me as he walked.

'What?' I stammered, choking on my food.

'Are you two like —'

'*No!*' I yelled.

Adam scuttled off past our table quickly, and Jason raised his eyebrows.

'Hey, cool it, man, I was just asking.'

'Well *don't. He* might be a gay freak but I'm not!' I left the table, knocking over a chair as I went.

Adam
He called me a gay freak. I left that cafeteria as fast as I could.

Miles
I didn't know what to do. I thought about following Adam, but I didn't. I took the long way round and went home, feeling absolutely disgusted with myself.

Back at home, I stood against the wall in my

room, breathing like I'd just run a marathon. At last I let myself be honest about my feelings. Adam meant the world to me.

Adam heard his train arriving at last. The low toot sounded eerie in the otherwise complete silence, and Adam found himself wondering if he could actually go through with it. He inched closer to the edge of the platform as the man with the long scarf and the old woman with the suitcase began to get up from their seats. He made an effort to control his deep breathing, hugging himself against the wind. The train approached from the distance, roaring along the tracks. Taking a shuddering breath, Adam hopped down from the platform to catch his train.

Miles stood at his station, becoming increasingly doubtful that his train would arrive. The screen said his train should leave at 17:55; it was already 18:05. *Perhaps it's been delayed*, he thought. He began to wonder if he should have caught it at the station near his house after all.

But they would have found and identified my body sooner that way.

Departure

Miles admitted defeat. He could tell the train wasn't coming, and started home.

Doesn't have to be today, after all.

To his utter surprise, he found himself stopping by Adam's house. I'm going to apologise, he decided. Apologise, and tell the truth once and for all – and if he laughs, I can see this through tomorrow.

Miles arrived at his friend's house soon after eight o'clock. With white, trembling hands he rang the bell and waited.

Innocent Deceit

Rebecca Pedelty

Innocent Deceit

A *heartbeat. Softly thudding*, racing against the clock. Distant, but coming closer, much closer. She watches the second-hand of the clock as it ticks. *Tick, tick.* Faster. *Thud, thud.* Closer. She grips the edge of the table, her body ravaged by anger, blood coursing through her veins, boiling. And she wonders: *What excuse this time?* She grimaces as she hears the quiet, familiar rumbling of thunder before the storm. She shivers and pulls her knees closer towards her chest, hugging herself. By now the heartbeat is deafening, like a thousand armies marching into battle. She covers her ears to block out their angry drumming. But they keep on, so hard that she nearly explodes. The thunder moves closer and becomes more frequent until she feels the clouds above her head, cracking in her ears.

Silence.

He walks in, soaking wet.

I was so angry, seething; I felt as if my skin was crawling. I didn't want to look at him, but I felt a magnetic pull towards him, something beyond my control that attracted me to him.

'Where have you been?' I whined. Even I could hear the pathetic tone in my voice and I thought to myself: Am I being unreasonable? Perhaps imagining things? But as he came closer I could smell it, the scent of some expensive perfume (one that I couldn't afford and he would never even think of buying me). It was on his clothes, his neck and his mouth. And all those feelings of doubt vanished. I glared at him with my arms folded over my chest.

I never thought we would end up like this. I knew he'd been with another woman, but I was so stupid, so scared of being alone, that I let it wash over me. I was clinging to him and I felt like a leech. He made me feel like that. My eyes were glowing a deep shade of jade green. He brushed me off and turned away.

'I'm sorry; I did say I would be working late. Jesus, Claire! Don't crowd me!' he snapped as I followed him into the bathroom like a desperate puppy dog.

'It's just I was worried. It's gone ten! You could have called to say you were going to be so much later than usual!' I said with my eyebrows raised. I felt a tinge of embarrassment as I realised I sounded exactly like my mother had once sounded.

'I've just got in. Give me a break, for Christ's sake. I'm starting to wonder . . . well . . . maybe it would be a good idea for us to . . .'

But I was already in the bedroom and could hardly make out what he was mumbling about. I smoothed down our fresh lilac quilt and went to draw the curtains. Through narrowed eyes, I looked out into the street as the rain lashed violently against the pavement; it glistened in the clinical orange light. It beat hard onto the pane, sending cascades of heavy showers down the glass. The window clouded over as my own vision blurred into a watery picture.

I felt it in my brain, a sharp jolt that spread to my heart and made my spine shiver. And then I knew. He couldn't leave me. I needed him.

My heart was racing again; my body tingling and I could taste electricity on my tongue. I could almost feel two heartbeats inside me. If I imagined hard enough, I could feel another life growing inside me. It would be perfect – the perfect solution to all my problems. If only it was true.

He swaggered in, rubbing his head with a clean towel and unbuttoning his shirt. He kicked off his soft leather shoes before stretching his tanned arms above his head and letting out a self-satisfied sigh.

'So, as I was saying . . .' he started again.

I closed my eyes and thought fast. If I said it out loud, it might come true. How naïve of me.

'Rob . . . I'm . . . pregnant,' I stuttered.

His jaw dropped and the world stood still for a split second.

I had promised myself from a very early age that I wouldn't turn out like my father. I knew how much he had hurt my mum when he left, and I never forgave him. Although recently, and it pained me to say it, I was starting to understand his reasons for leaving.

My feelings had once been very strong. I had loved Claire more than I'd ever loved anyone – and in a way I still did. But the cruel claw of temptation grasped me tightly. I felt engulfed, suffocated, and I couldn't break free.

I'd been having an affair for a few months now and the bitter irony was that I didn't even love the girl. It was simply sex; a classic escape from my normal life, which I was drifting further and further away from. Looking back, I felt sick.

But a baby, this was too much. I felt my jaw drop to the floor when I heard her say it. This changed everything, as just a few minutes ago I was thinking of ending our relationship. The lying and deceiving was eating me up, and I was finding it hard to look at myself in the mirror seriously, let alone look into Claire's eyes.

'Well, what do you think?' she asked me, timidly. I could hear her heart beat from the other side of the room and I could tell from her expression that she was as petrified as I was. I took a deep breath, walked over to her, and held her in my arms.

When he held me like that I felt warm, secure, and safe. For a moment, the rain stopped and I was floating in a halcyon sea. I felt surrounded by light and my heartrate slowed. I could have stayed like that for ever, in his embrace, where I was protected from everything else. We were so close we could have merged into one body, and I knew that he was there for me, just me. But the harsh reality of it all was that I was losing my grip, trying to cling on to every last breath, every last moment – and he was slipping through my fingers like sand fast escaping in a dry desert, like the storm that sweeps through uncontrollably, leaving it barren. My hourglass was running out.

It was Rob who pulled away first. His answer to my question was unexpected, but it left me with a sense of fulfilment. As he rested his hand on my stomach and gently rubbed it, I felt myself drifting calmly into a state of euphoria. He was smiling a smile I'd never seen before; it almost looked forced, and I could see the anxiety in his eyes.

In hindsight, I realised how ridiculous the situation really was. I had always been shocked at how he could lie to me about where he'd been, what he'd been doing. Although I had accepted it, I could never understand how he managed his conscience. Now, here I was, doing exactly the same thing, lying to him, deceiving him. But as long as I believed that it was for a good reason, I could convince myself it wasn't lying. I could hear the ticking, endless ticking, thudding in my heart. When would this feeling go away?

'Of course I'm shocked, but you know I'd do anything for a baby, Claire!'

He sounded so sincere, and I knew then that this wasn't how it should be. This was meant to be one of the happiest moments of our lives. A new life! A tiny baby growing inside me that was only ours, something that belonged exclusively to us.

Somehow though, it's not the same when it's fake.

'You don't sound very pleased,' she whispered.

I knew what she meant and she was right. My cheeks were aching as I forced myself to look happy. I tried to pull myself together, act like a human being. It was a tiny baby, which belonged to us. It was part of me, mine. What was wrong with me? I couldn't get rid of this sheer sense of anxiety. I felt a pulling at my brain and realised I had to do something. My pain was sharp and intense, so I leaned over to kiss her. She looked so blissful, almost unhealthily happy. The more we kissed, the stronger my pain became, and I couldn't take it any more.

We went to bed together that night, for the first time in weeks. I don't know what we were trying to prove, but I felt numb. My brain was frozen and my body felt rigid, as if it didn't belong to me any more. I had been taken over, and I felt as if my life had been stolen, stolen by her.

A few weeks passed and the baby became the core of

my thoughts, of my life. Although it was constantly in my mind I could never talk about it. 'It' became an awkward subject, like somebody's death. How sick was that? My exterior was the caring father, persistently asking Claire how she was, trying to look after her. But I heard nothing she said, ignored her replies and blocked out her feelings. I was going through it all alone – and it was hell. I was almost giving myself reverse psychology, making myself believe so firmly that I cared, that I was happy.

This was exactly what I had wanted; Rob had become my ideal man, consumed by me, by our baby. My plan had worked so incredibly.

But, I never realised how just three weeks would feel like three hundred pregnancies over and over again. The guilt would physically torture me inside, and every day I was on the verge of telling him the truth. My nightmares were filled with horrors of him finding out. The images in my dreams were so real, of disfigured babies and myself hollowed out from the inside. It was ripping me apart. I'd wake up every night in a cold sweat, screaming. Rob was always there to comfort and soothe me back to sleep. I'd close my eyes, feeling his body around me, and see black.

All day long it was relentlessly on my mind, scorching my

brain so I could honestly no longer remember the reasons I had for doing this. I was going insane.

It was a month after it all happened when Rob came home early from work again. He walked over to me and kissed my cheek and had a huge grin on his face. I hadn't noticed that he was carrying a bag until he handed it to me. I smiled at him.

'What's this?'

'Just look, I know it's way too early, but I couldn't resist,' he said, beaming. As he walked away I looked in the bag. A bolt of lightning severed me in two and I threw the contents of the bag on the floor. It was then that I cracked. I collapsed on to the sofa and burst into tears; I grabbed the baby clothes and ripped at them. Rob came rushing in as usual.

'What is it? What's the matter?' He was as frantic as I was.

I put my head on his chest and sobbed, and I just couldn't help myself. I told him the truth – everything, the bitter and twisted truth.

I picked up the bag and threw it at her. I felt liberation a driving force inside, and I was out of the door and into the street without looking back.

* * *

A heartbeat. Softly thudding, racing against the clock. Distant, but coming closer, much closer. She watches the second-hand of the clock as it ticks. *Tick, tick.* Faster. *Thud, thud.* Closer. She is sitting on the edge of the bath, a pregnancy test in her hand, shuddering uncontrollably. She hears a second heartbeat. She closes her eyes and hears the familiar drumming.

She blinks.

It's positive.

Basketball

Alison Ritchie

Basketball

'No.'

It was out of her mouth before she had time to think. She didn't consider the reasons, or consequences, or anything. It was a 'no' of pure instinct.

Miranda frowned. 'No?' She didn't sound like she believed it. It probably wasn't something she heard very often.

After all, everyone wanted to go round to Miranda's house. Holly knew the other girls all thought her lucky. She was the second most popular girl in school, Miranda's chosen friend. None of them understood.

Alison Ritchie

None of them understood what it was like to be alone with Miranda. To have Miranda watch them with her judging eyes. To see Miranda sit back, demanding entertainment. None of them understood how Holly felt, when her jokes failed, when her mouth went dry and all she could hear was Miranda's mocking laugh.

Holly didn't know why Miranda liked her. She didn't know why anyone liked her. Inside, she always felt scared and tense, knowing that any slip or mistake would be seen and paid for. Around Miranda, around her friends, she could never relax.

The idea of spending an extra five hours alone with Miranda, who always knew exactly the right words to hurt and humiliate Holly, made Holly feel slightly sick. 'I'm sorry,' she said. 'I can't.'

'You can't come round mine? Why not?' Miranda demanded.

'Because . . .' She paused, excuses flittering across her brain, all sounding as silly as the last. She couldn't tell Miranda the truth. She couldn't even imagine what the consequences would be. In the corner of her eye, she could see some boys playing on the playground. 'Basketball!' she cried. 'I'm on a basketball team, and that's when we meet! So I'll be busy. I'm sorry.'

Miranda's eyes narrowed, but she didn't ask anything else. Instead, when the bell rang, she ran over to some other girls. Holly felt relieved to see her go.

It wasn't until a few days later that the trouble started – and even when it did, she didn't realise it at first. She was in the cloakroom, sorting out her shoes, when Steph came and sat beside her.

'I didn't know you played basketball, Holly,' she said, searching through her bag.

"Basketball?' It took Holly a moment to remember. 'Oh! Yes. Basketball. Well, I only started quite recently,' she lied smoothly.

'Where d'you play?'

Holly hesitated. What should she say? 'The leisure centre?' she offered. That was right, wasn't it? They must play basketball at the leisure centre.

Steph frowned, but nodded, and said nothing else.

Leaning back against the wall, Holly wished she wasn't quite so hot and sweaty, but felt thankful for her narrow escape.

But later that day at lunch, when she approached her friends, she was surprised to see them turn away. 'What?' she asked, thinking it was a game. 'What's up?'

One of them giggled, and another muttered, 'Just ignore her.' Jessica turned, her blue eyes spiteful.

'Give it up, Holly,' she said. 'We know you're a liar.'

'Yeah,' chimed in another, 'Miranda and Steph have told us everything!'

Miranda and Steph? What would Miranda be doing with a girl like Steph? Steph wasn't cool. But as Holly's friends continued to watch her, she felt her skin growing cold.

Jessica smirked. 'We know all about it,' she told Holly. 'Miranda told us about how you lied to her about playing basketball. But Steph's brother plays at the leisure centre, and he says he's never seen you there!'

'But . . . but . . .' Steph's brother played there? Horrified, Holly remembered the other girl's questions that morning.

All her friends were laughing now, eyes greedy as they drank in her shame. One of them started chanting under her breath, 'Liar! Liar!'

'Yeah,' another sniggered. 'Is your name really Holly, or did you lie about that too?'

Unable to bear it, Holly spun around, planning to storm away. But what she saw across the playground made her freeze. Sitting together on a bench, like they'd been best friends all their lives: Steph and Miranda, Steph leaning over to whisper in Miranda's ear.

Steph watched coolly when Holly discovered the woodlice in her pencil case and jumped up with a scream. Sitting beside Steph, Miranda descended into giggles, leaning against Steph's shoulder. Steph laughed too.

They'd been torturing Holly for days now: taunts in assembly, rubbish in her bag, food stolen from her lunch box, stickers on her back, and chants of 'Liar, liar, pants on fire!' whenever she spoke. Steph wondered how much more of it Holly could stand. Holly had already run off to the toilets crying three times that week, and it was only Wednesday.

Steph couldn't care too much. At least Holly now knew how it felt. All her life, Steph had been the smart one, the one who did her homework, who never got in trouble. The one who never got invited to any parties.

Holly, on the other hand, had always had everything Steph wanted. She'd always had friends to whisper with, and fashionable clothes to be admired. Best of all, she'd sat next to Miranda. Steph had asked Holly round to play at her house once. Holly had laughed in her face and then told all her friends. They'd laughed too.

Steph didn't even feel sympathy when, at break, Holly finally broke down in tears for a fourth time, running into the cloakroom. For years, Steph had thrown up every morning because she'd been so scared of coming to school. So scared of school – and people like Holly Jacobs. Well, now Holly could see what it was like. Now Steph was the popular one, the one Miranda liked. Holly was nothing, and it was all her own fault. She shouldn't have been caught lying.

Steph frowned in annoyance as someone tugged at her coat. She turned to see her brother's podgy face scowling up at her. Her brother, who had never played basketball in his life.

'Can I have my money now?' he whined, without waiting for her to speak.

'No!' she snapped. 'I told you, you have to wait till we get our pocket money on Friday!'

He pouted sulkily. 'But we're going to the shop this afternoon! And I did what you said, I told them I played basketball!'

'So? Look, if you go away, I'll give you more!'

'How much?'

Steph bit her lip, thinking. She had a bit saved up, but Miranda wanted to go swimming on Saturday . . . 'One pound more. Think of all the chocolate you could buy with that!'

His grin was the only agreement she got, before he ran back across the concrete towards his friends. Steph watched him go. It had been easy, she reflected, getting him to lie for her. He hadn't even asked what she wanted him to say before agreeing. He'd seen the sweets dancing in his head, and become her willing slave. *But a greedy slave*, she thought with a frown. He kept asking for more and more money, and she had to give it to him. She couldn't risk him telling Miranda she had lied.

She heard a shriek of laughter from the cloakroom doors, and turned to see Miranda backing away from someone. Holly, Steph decided. Who else?

Her spirits lifted as Miranda spotted her, and walked over with a wave. People turned as she passed and saw she was headed for Steph. Steph glowed with pride. *Finally*, she thought. Finally, she was popular. And Miranda would never suspect a thing.

Steph grinned as Miranda linked her arm through hers, and they stepped around the edge of the playground. The other girls watched in envy, and Holly was nowhere to be seen. Miranda gave her a bright smile. 'Want to come round mine tonight?'

Steph didn't think before saying, 'Yes.'

The Versatility of Maria

Jasmine Singh

The Versatility of Maria

On such a cold winter's night you would expect families to be warm and cosy in their loving homes, sitting by a log fire, drinking a cup of cocoa or a big glass of red wine. You could imagine that in Acacia Avenue, with its perfectly uniform mock Tudor houses, where people had no less than two and no more than three cars – one of which had to be a BMW or a Mercedes and one a 4x4, even though every road was flat and there wasn't a hill to be seen within a ten-mile radius. Little children in their Dolce & Gabbana trainers (possibly purchased from eBay) were looking out on to their snow-covered gardens where the snow lay so perfectly that even the cat didn't dare to leave pawprints.

Every house on Acacia Avenue fitted this description apart from one: number twenty-seven. This was, indeed, like all the others in appearance: a perfect garden, two cars; but the only thing different about this house was what was going on inside. Peter and Maria had lived in number twenty-seven Acacia Avenue with their dog for about a year now. They were not married, but they were a couple, and everyone in Acacia Avenue knew them as a happy couple. They both had good careers. Peter was a successful lawyer; Maria was a senior marketer for an investment bank and frequently travelled around the world. This was the only way in which Maria did not fit the mould of the women in Acacia Avenue, who were, in the main, stereotypical middle-class housewives who split their time between looking after their families, trips to the beautician and weekly coffee mornings where most of the serious gossiping took place.

This night, in number twenty-seven it was cold outside and even colder inside. No fire was lit; no lights could be seen; the house was in darkness and there was an eerie feeling around this property. If you had been looking through the garden window into the kitchen, just a few hours ago you would have seen Peter and Maria. You would have thought that the happy couple were just about to sit down to eat a delicious meal that had been lovingly prepared by Maria. Indeed, Maria had prepared lamb casserole, Peter's favourite dish. Maria was an excellent cook and, when she could fit it into her hectic work schedule, had dinner parties to which various neighbours were invited.

However, tonight was to prove to be no ordinary night. Tonight was the night Maria would announce to Peter that she had been having an affair, and was going to leave him and start a new life with someone she had met whilst working in Sweden sometime last year.

Right now, if you had been looking through the kitchen window, you would have seen Peter standing very still with a knife in his hand. The only sound to be heard was the kitchen clock: *tick tock*, *tick tock*. Maria lay slumped on the floor. There is no twist to this story; Peter killed Maria.

Peter stood there staring, just staring at the lifeless

body on the floor. He was not one to panic though, even in a situation like this. Immediately, his brain began to work; he put the knife in the state-of-the-art dishwasher and set it to wash. He knew what he was going to do. Peter had to hide the evidence – and the biggest piece of evidence was, of course, Maria's body. He first drew all the curtains and blinds so nobody could look into the house. So too bad if you were standing in the garden looking in – your view would now be blocked. He then locked the dog in the bedroom, as he knew the dog would know what was going on, and the dog already disliked him.

Peter dragged the body down to the basement, trying not to trip on the stairs on the way. She was far heavier than she looked. He locked the door behind him. The basement was where Peter kept all his tools and his 'special' set of knives that he only used on rare occasions. The basement was also where the large chest freezer was. Maria, being such a keen cook, needed a lot of freezer space to store her various concoctions.

It was a few weeks before any of the neighbours acknowledged Maria's absence. Due to the heavy

The Versatility of Maria

snow recently, the coffee mornings had not been as frequent. When the neighbours did at last remark to Peter that they had not seen Maria for a while, Peter told them straight that she had been having an affair and had run off with her Swedish lover.

Peter carried on his life, like nothing had happened, and people were touched that he was putting on such a brave face. All the neighbours in Acacia Avenue – being the good neighbours that they were – rallied round, and Peter was never short of a dinner invitation. No one was insensitive enough to ask any more questions about Maria; they all knew what career girls were like: all briefcase and no knickers. They all convinced themselves that Peter was better off without the trollop and they had all seen this coming.

Months went by. Peter decided to have a dinner party and invited most of the neighbours, to return the hospitality that they had been kind enough to extend to him.

On the night of Peter's dinner party, everyone was in high spirits (which may have been something to do with the strong spirits in everyone's glasses). Peter put on a CD called *Classical Music for Dinner Parties*; he had the whole collection: *Classical Music for Long Journeys*, *Classical Music for Relaxing*, *Classical Music for Gardening*, and *Classical Music for Sleeping*. He never really liked classical music, but Maria had loved it.

It was a lovely spring evening and the French doors leading out to the back garden were wide open. People admired the new herb garden. Peter's response was simple: if it wasn't for Maria, the herbs would not have flourished. She always said that good fertilisers were the key to good plants. In fact, Maria had fertilised this particular patch exceedingly well. Peter smirked to himself as he plucked a handful of parsley for the casserole that was simmering in the kitchen and was to form the main course.

The dinner party was a great success. Everyone commented on how beautifully the table was laid out and especially on the unusual leather tablemats with the strange tassels. They questioned him about where they were from. His answers were effortless: they were just something he picked up on his travels some years ago. He never did remember what animal they were from. Peter stroked one of the tablemats and could not help thinking Maria had always had lovely smooth silky hair and such soft skin.

The Versatility of Maria

The intoxicating aromas that were emanating from the kitchen soon materialised in a large casserole dish. Everyone tucked in and was secretly surprised at Peter's culinary skills. When asked about the recipe he could not recall the exact ingredients, but he just said that Maria's heart had gone into developing it. She always was a superb cook, and this dish reminded him so much of her that it was almost as if she were there with him. The plates would have been licked clean if people's manners had not kicked in.

After people had eaten to contentment, everyone made their way back to their own homes, where they could be heard remarking how well Peter had coped – almost as if Maria had never left.

Strangely enough, the dog developed a great affection for Peter. Maybe it was because the dog felt Peter's loss, or maybe it was something to do with the juicy bones that found their way to the dog, a supply of which Peter kept in the freezer.

The Lie-Like-Life

Saranja Sivachelvam

The Lie-Like-Life

My life is a lie; I live a lie; I am a lie. 'Yes, Linda is a pleasant child to have in the class,' my teacher says. 'She sits quietly and gets on with her work' is another common comment. 'Oh, Linda is extremely polite and gets along with everyone.' That one just makes me sick.

I, Linda Mackiness, am not a very outgoing person. Even in my younger years, all I ever heard was, 'Be nice to all your little friends, Linda!' And, believe it or not, I was. I was, I still am, and I will be.

I was always the goody-girl in my class. The class

idol. Me? Yeah right. No way. Not if they knew what I really thought, deep down inside. I'm very good at bottling things up inside myself.

So, I say I live a lie, but what is a day in that lie-like-life actually like?

Well, I get up at seven a.m. in the morning. I hate getting up at seven; I would rather get up at eight, but I told everyone that I liked getting up at seven. I was being nice, so I had to lie. Great, my first lie of the morning. Next, I brush my teeth, and wash my face, and get into my school uniform. We are allowed to choose what we want to wear – skirt or trousers. I wear a skirt, although I hate wearing skirts – I much prefer trousers – but I wear a skirt because everyone else thinks I look cute in a skirt so, to be polite, I wear one. My second lie of the morning. Then comes breakfast. I am given a bowl of Kelloggs cornflakes with milk and slices of banana. I hate slices of banana in my cereal, but to be nice, I say it tastes good. Lie number three. Three lies and I have yet to get to school.

I reach school, and I have to wait ten cold minutes outside. I told my parents that I didn't mind waiting, but really I do, because I wear a skirt, and it is extremely chilly, especially when it is snowing. Lie number four – I'm doing fabulously, aren't I? Already you can see why I say that I live a lie-like-life, can't you? I mean, all these lies – who said my life wasn't one?

As soon as I enter school I go to my locker, and, on the way, I see a food technology teacher. I wish him a 'Good morning', inside thinking: *What is so good about spending eight hours a day with selfish, egotistic, self-absorbed teenagers?* I compliment him on his choice of clothes for the day, inside actually thinking to myself: *Who would wear such a combination?* – which is really evil, but he is a really nice person after all. So what does it matter? Anyway, that is still lie number five. Remember, class has yet to start.

So, at eight-fifty my first lesson starts. I try to look eager at the prospect of going to some dreaded lesson and, as usual, my fellow, slightly dense, homosapiens translate my look of boredom as enthusiasm. But, isn't that the point? I'm being nice to my teacher by not making it clear that I am literally going to fall asleep in his/her lesson. And so, in this way, my lessons pass until period three, after which is break. During break, I have to endure the pain of various friends telling me the joys of their morning. I pretend to be giving them my full attention, but inside I'm really thinking: *You awful, self-obsessed people! Do you not have anything better to do?*

I *am* nice to my friends, but inside I'm thinking: *Girl, that hairstyle so does not suit you.* Of course, I don't exactly say that; in fact, I just say that her new way of doing up her hair might catch on as the latest trend. God forbid another ten girls coming into school with a crow's nest – sorry, a bundle of hair – on their heads! But, I *do* try to be nice on the outside. I mean, *I'm* nice little Linda Mackiness, so what could *I* possibly do wrong?

I rush to fourth period as soon as possible, in order to wash my hands of such tedious and annoying company. But fourth period starts with the usual drone of a teacher, my Italian teacher. He is not a bad teacher, but let's just say he's more powerful than the average sleeping pill. That's how boring he is. And guess what? What else? I told him I thought he was wonderful, and that geography was one of my favourite subjects. Not.

Periods five and six whizz by – I wish. I've told all my teachers that I like them and that they're doing a good job of teaching us – the Laws of Boredom, that is, and the different ways of falling asleep. If it weren't for one particular teacher, I wouldn't have learned how to sit up and sleep at the same time.

After periods five and six comes lunch; I wait for a friend and then, together, we rush downstairs to the lunch room. It being a Monday, we both had Youth Choir to attend at one-thirty p.m. We hurriedly ate our way through our sandwiches and ran to the choir rehearsal – we made it just in time. I told my guitar teacher that I liked singing, just to be nice, but she decided to ask me to join the choir. Now, I don't really mind singing, it's just the rehearsal. But I told everyone I like rehearsals, so I can't do anything about it. But hey, all my lies back-stab me, don't they?

Periods seven and eight are like paradise – I dream about going home at last. Finally! Another cluster of my polite, just-to-be-nice comments and lies come forth, but these ones don't matter because I'm going home! Three-forty p.m. – YES! Alleluia! Now, I can really let out my feelings into my journal, and look back at my day today. My life, the perfect lie, the tongue twister – my lie-like-life. It doesn't get any better.

The Businessman

Conrad Steel

The Businessman

lie (laɪ), n.

1. A false statement deliberately presented as being true;
a falsehood.

2. Something meant to deceive or give a wrong
impression.

Walter Feininger was a businessman. Or at least,
he seemed like a businessman; he was a business-like
man. In any case, he was a man who liked business.
Unfortunately, Walter Feininger didn't have any.
Which was why he was broke.

But there could be no doubt that he was still a businessman. It was in the way he moved, the way he spoke, the way he dressed, the way he breathed. It was in his firm-but-not-too-firm handshake. It was in his self-assured glance when he entered a room. Being a businessman was in Walter Feininger's soul.

For him, the exact type of business was unimportant. He had previously founded a small, independent ceramics firm, wedging himself in as a middle man between the factories and the customers, but after a few years the metaphorical big kids had pushed him over and stolen his lunch-money, leaving him, as he delicately put it, 'having a rest between jobs'. But even in the absence of anything resembling business, Walter Feininger still considered himself to be, in essence, a businessman.

However, a businessman needs to sell things, and in order to do that he needs to buy things, and in order to do that he must have money – and this was a qualification that Walter Feininger could not claim to possess. Luckily for him, though, he knew a man that did. He had a cousin, a little older than him, who through no particular virtue of his own had inherited a small fortune from some successful but childless uncle on the non-Feininger side of the family. The cousin was now in charge of a couple of local art galleries and hardly touched his undeserved cash, so it seemed to Walter that he would be delighted to use a little of it to back any well-thought-out business venture of a needy relative that might come his way.

Walter had never been especially close to this particular cousin, but he always saw him at least once a year, so he did not feel it in the least bit awkward to phone him up and arrange a meeting. The cousin was warily noncommittal, but for all that Walter Feininger was rather the family's black sheep and by all accounts not entirely reliable when it came to money, he was still a relative and blood ties demanded that the proposal be at least given a hearing.

So on the day of the meeting, the cousin sat in the restaurant in which they had arranged to meet, thinking how most tactfully to refuse Walter's scheme. He had heard the Chinese whisper that Walter's last venture had collapsed after only a couple of months and that he was now on the brink of bankruptcy, and for all that blood is thicker than water, the density of both pales in comparison to that of cold, hard currency. Yet when Walter arrived, the cousin realised that he must have been misinformed. This was no down-and-out tramp. This was a role model to raise one's children by, full of vim, vigour, and other equally desirable substances. This was a high priest of the gods of commerce. This was a businessman. The expensive suit and shiny shoes left over from the days of Feininger Ceramics Ltd., the handshake, the confident eye-contact, the walk, the talk: they spoke to the cousin in a voice incomparably louder than untrustworthy words. 'Your money will be in completely safe hands here . . .' 'Trust me . . .' 'There's no way that you can lose, really . . .' 'Trust me . . .' 'A one hundred and fifty per cent return is almost guaranteed . . .' 'Trust me trust me trust me trust me trust . . .' Walter Feininger said all of these things, and his lips never moved. Walter lied to his cousin, and the lie was perfect, because perfection in a lie is that it really goes without saying.

Walter's plan was really just a repeat of his ceramics project. The area of commerce would of course have to be different – he fancied that he might try his hand in computer sales – but the basics of the business would remain the same. He had learned a little from his previous mistakes, and he was sure that he would pick up any necessary expertise as he went along. His cousin was at first a little concerned that Walter seemed to know absolutely nothing about the area into which he planned to launch himself, but the shiny shoes said: *What do little details like that matter? This is business, and I'm a businessman. What more do you want?* Dazzled by Walter's charm, suavity and footwear, the cousin's doubts evaporated one by one. He didn't notice them leaving, and didn't realise when they were gone, but gradually he became conscious that this was not a man to distrust: this was a businessman. He was slowly deceived by each one of Walter's little lies of movement and attitude – the miniature shakes of the head, the relaxed twitches of the mouth, the angle of the feet – and every one of these lies was perfect, because perfection in a lie is that no one even notices it's been told.

Walter Feininger was never a religious man, being a confirmed sceptic both by nature and by nurture, but if any superstition resided in the portion of the brain usually reserved for awe of a higher being, it was a belief in Business. Of course, it was, for him, a profession – except during this very temporary embarrassment that had, through absolutely no fault of his own, befallen him – but it was more than this. It was a way of life, it was a state of mind. Naturally, it was also the pursuit of those two elusive unicorns of modern motivation: Money and Happiness; but somehow for Walter, it had evolved past that stage. His cousin believed that he was a businessman. A businessman is a man who does business. Walter, at that moment, was not a man who did business. And yet, Walter Feininger was a businessman . . .

So Walter got his loan, and was grateful for it. He used it to set up Cassius Computers Ltd., and this time he inserted his wedge as a middle man rather more firmly, and for all that his rivals pushed at him, they couldn't dislodge him. He picked up the expertise that he needed, and he became quite a well-known figure in the business world. Over the years, as the company flourished, the cousin got his one hundred and fifty per cent return, and considerably more (because perfection in a lie is that it benefits even those that it is told to). And Walter Feininger retired on his sixty-fifth birthday, every inch the businessman – as, really, he always had been. Although on the day that he met his cousin in an upmarket Italian restaurant to have their little talk he cannot strictly be said to have been a man in business, he had always, very definitely, been a businessman. The perfect lie, in the end, isn't really a lie at all.

Other books from Piccadilly Press

Sea Girls

The Crystal City

j.g. elliot

*As Polly dived into the pool, the water went straight up
her nose. Normally this would make her choke and gasp for
air, but this time some instinct made her suck the water
through her nose and push it out of her mouth. She could
breathe underwater!*

Even before this, Polly had always felt different. But
then she finds a kindred spirit in Lisa who she meets at
a swimming competition. The two girls discover that
they both have the same fish-shaped birthmark, were
both adopted, and can both breathe underwater. Surely
it can't just be coincidence?

When a strong current drags them to the depths of the
ocean, they not only discover their true identities, but
an amazing world – more incredible and more
disturbing than they could ever have imagined . . .

Venus Spring

Stunt★Girl

JONNY ZUCKER

Venus leaped from the platform like a springing cheetah pumping her legs in mid-air as she'd seen long-jumpers do. There were gasps from people below – there was no way she could make it across without the rope. She hung in the air as if for a second she'd bypassed the laws of time and gravity.

Venus Spring is fourteen and this is the first summer she's been allowed to go to stunt camp. It is a dream come true, something she has been working towards for years. But while she is there, she stumbles on a devious and terrifying plot that threatens the surrounding countryside, and Venus is determined to uncover it.

BEST
OF
FRIENDS

True stories of
friendships that
blossomed or bombed

As told to
Sophie Parkin

Friendship can be better than falling in love.

'Some days my jaw would ache from having laughed so
much.' Cathy Hopkins, writer

Or it can break your heart

'I was suddenly terrified that all of our friendship had
been one great big lie.' Flic

And some friendships stay with you forever

'She started to crop up in my dreams, and I did in hers.
And that's when we got back in touch again.'
Sophie Ellis-Bextor, singer

Sophie Parkin has talked to teenage girls and
high-profile women about the friendships which have
meant the most to them. Their stories - affectionate and
angry, bittersweet and tragic - show just how much our
lives are shaped by our best friends.

Things ☽
I Know
About
Love

KATE LE VANN

Things I know about love.

*1. People don't always tell you the truth
about how they feel.*

*2. Nothing that happens between two people
is guaranteed to be private.*

*3. I don't know if you ever get over having
your heart broken.*

Livia's experience of love has been disappointing, to
say the least. But all that is about to change. After
years of illness, she's off to spend the summer with her
brother in America. She's making up for lost time,
and she's writing it all down in her private blog.

America is everything she'd dreamed of – and then
she meets Adam. Can Livia put her past behind
her and risk falling in love again?